Candy Cove Pirates

ROSIE BANKS

This is the Secret Kingdom

Candy Cove

Book
One

Book
One

Contents

A Sweet Village

"These colouring books are great," said Ellie Macdonald, holding up one with a skull-and-crossbones flag on the cover.

"Connor's crazy about pirates," Summer Hammond said. "He keeps making all his toys walk the plank!"

Connor was one of Summer's little brothers. His pirate-themed birthday party was tomorrow and he and Summer's youngest brother, Finn, could hardly wait for it to begin! Summer and her best friends, Ellie and Jasmine, were in Summer's bedroom putting the party bags together.

"These eye patches are good, too," Jasmine Smith said, putting one on. "Arr, shiver me timbers!"

Ellie laughed, making her red curls bob around her face. "All you need now is a wooden leg and you'll be a perfect pirate." She put the colouring book into the party bag she was filling.

"Look!" gasped Summer suddenly, pointing towards her wardrobe.

Ellie and Jasmine turned and saw a silvery glow shining out of the narrow gap between the wardrobe doors.

"The Magic Box!" Jasmine cried.

The three girls shared a wonderful secret. They looked after a wooden box carved with mermaids and unicorns and other wonderful creatures. But it wasn't just any box, it was magic! It could take them to an amazing land called the Secret Kingdom, where brownies, unicorns, pixies and other wonderful

creatures lived, ruled by kind King Merry.
The girls had visited lots of times to help
solve the problems caused by Queen
Malice, the king's horrid sister. She was
always trying to take over her brother's
kingdom and make everyone in it
miserable.

Summer threw
open her wardrobe
and took out the
wooden box. The
mirror on the lid
was shining with
silver light.

"I hope Queen
Malice isn't
causing trouble
again," Ellie said
anxiously.

"If she is, we'll soon stop her," Jasmine said determinedly.

Summer put the box on her bed and they all gathered round. She held her breath as a riddle appeared in the mirror and Ellie read it out:

"Dear friends, please come to
somewhere sweet
To share a Secret Kingdom treat.
You'll find this village near the sea.
Just call its name to summon me!"

The box lid flew open and a sheet of paper floated out. It was a map of the Secret Kingdom with figures moving across it. "Look at the unicorns," said Summer, pointing to three creatures galloping through a green valley, their colourful tails streaming out behind them.

"Let's look along the coast," Jasmine said. "Remember, we're searching for a village, somewhere sweet…"

"Fancy Dress Village, where everyone dressed up in those amazing costumes, was full of sweet little cottages," said Summer thoughtfully, "but it wasn't near the sea."

"There!" Jasmine cried. "That village is next to the water and it's called Candy Cove! That sounds *really* sweet."

"It must be the place," agreed Ellie.

The girls exchanged excited looks. "The answer is Candy Cove!" they cried together.

There was a brilliant flash of pink light, then golden sparkles came whooshing out of the box and whirled round Summer's bedroom. As the sparkles slowed, the girls saw a beautiful pixie with messy blonde hair riding on a leaf. "Trixi!" they exclaimed.

"It's *so* lovely to see you again," Trixi cried, beaming at them. She zoomed up to each of the girls and kissed them on the very tips of their noses.

"It's great to see you, too," said Summer.

"What a gorgeous outfit, Trixi," said Ellie. The little pixie was wearing a pink-and-white striped dress. Her hat and shoes were candy coloured, too, and her hat was a swirl with a cherry on the top that reminded Ellie of ice cream!

"Thank you!" Trixi twirled round on her leaf. "Are you ready for another trip to the Secret Kingdom?"

"You bet!" cried Jasmine.

"Has Queen Malice done something horrible?" Summer asked anxiously.

"Not this time, thank goodness," Trixi said. "King Merry and I just wanted you to meet Mrs Sherbet."

"Who's Mrs Sherbet?" asked Ellie.

"She's in charge of the Secret Kingdom Sweet Shop," explained Trixi with a smile. "One of the kingdom's most delicious traditions!"

Jasmine licked her lips. This all sounded very exciting!

"The Sweet Shop only appears once a year, in summer. Mrs Sherbet travels all around the kingdom for a week, sharing treats with everyone," continued Trixi. "And best of all, the Sweet Shop looks different every time. Last year it was shaped like a giant hot-air balloon and this year it's a magnificent ship – The Sweet Princess! The whole ship is made

from delicious things to eat!"

"I can't wait to see it," Jasmine said, grinning at Ellie and Summer.

"Let's go!" Trixi cried. "Mrs Sherbet can't go around the kingdom until she and King Merry have performed the launch ceremony. This year it has to be held at precisely midday when the tide is at its very highest. That way the ship has a brilliant start on its journey around the Secret Kingdom, taking a year's worth of sweets to everyone!"

Hurriedly the girls held hands. Trixi tapped her magic ring and chanted:

"Take us as quickly as can be,
To Candy Cove beside the sea!"

A sparkling whirlwind whooshed out

of the Magic Box and lifted the girls off their feet. It smelled of toffee and humbugs, making their mouths water.

"Wheee!" cried Summer. "Secret Kingdom, here we come!"

A moment later they landed with a gentle bump in an old-fashioned little village. The street was lined with shops and workshops with red-and-white striped awnings, and cottages with

thatched roofs and brightly coloured
front doors.

"Let's look at the workshops while we
wait for King Merry to arrive," suggested
Trixi. "All of Mrs Sherbet's sweet treats
are made in Candy Cove, then they
will be loaded on to the Sweet Princess,
ready to travel around the kingdom to be
shared with everyone!"

The first workshop was called Cookie

Corner. As the girls ran to peer into the window, Summer spotted her reflection in the glass. "We're wearing our tiaras again," she said with a smile.

Their beautiful jewelled tiaras always appeared when the girls arrived. They showed that they were Very Special Friends of the Secret Kingdom. Ellie and Jasmine grinned. It was so good to be back!

Inside the workshop, gnomes with long white beards and colourful, pointed hats were mixing ingredients together in big bowls. While the girls watched, a gnome opened an oven and took out a tray of golden cookies.

The workshop door opened and another smiling gnome came scurrying out with a plate heaped with a pile of glittering butterfly-shaped biscuits.

"Catch-me Cookies for the Special Friends of the Secret Kingdom!" he cried, holding the plate out to the girls.

"Thanks!" Jasmine exclaimed.

"But why are they called Catch-me Cookies?" Summer asked.

Trixi giggled. "You'll see."

As the girls reached for a biscuit, the cookies fluttered into the air! Laughing, Summer, Ellie and Jasmine chased after the flying biscuits, jumping up until they'd

all caught one each.

"Wow!" cried Ellie, taking a bite.
"These are yummy!"

Nibbling their biscuits, they hurried
to the next workshop, Pancake Place,
where pancakes sizzled on a long stove.
Suddenly, there was a bright flash and
the pancakes flipped over. When both
sides were cooked,
they flipped
themselves
again and a
young gnome
raced over to
catch them
on a plate.
"I wonder if
he ever misses
any," Summer

giggled, as another gnome piled delicious strawberries and cream on top of the pancakes.

The friends moved outside. "Where shall we go next?" Ellie asked excitedly.

"I wonder what they make there?" asked Jasmine, peering in a nearby window. Inside, the workshop was filled with clouds of white powder and all the gnomes were covered in it from head to toe.

"Sizzling sherbet," said Trixi, flying her leaf over to them. "It's made from—" She broke off suddenly as a loud noise rang out above them.

"*AHHHCOO!*" the sound echoed around the cobbled streets of the quiet village.

As the girls looked up, they saw dark

clouds appearing in the sky.

"Oh no!" Ellie gasped. "Stormclouds."

The girls looked at each other in alarm. "It must be Queen Malice and the Storm Sprites!" Summer cried.

The Sweet Princess

As the girls looked up at the sky
nervously, the clouds parted and a
beautiful rainbow appeared. Then King
Merry came whizzing down it!

"It was only King Merry!" Jasmine
laughed in relief.

King Merry sneezed and the sound echoed around the clouds, making the loud noise they'd heard. "Thank goodness!" Summer exclaimed, feeling very happy it wasn't the mean queen, who often travelled around the kingdom on a thunder cloud.

The little king landed in a heap at the bottom of the rainbow slide and gave a sneeze so big that his crown and glasses flew off and his purple cloak flapped over his head. "Help! Where am I?" he gasped. "Who turned out the lights!"

The girls ran forward to help him. Ellie and Summer untangled him from his cloak and helped him to his feet, while Jasmine picked up his crown and glasses.

"Thank you," said King Merry, sniffing. "I think some sizzling sherbet went up my nose." He put on his glasses and then beamed. "Why, it's Ellie, Jasmine and Summer! How delightful to see you all."

"We're very glad to be here, Your Majesty," Ellie said with a grin.

King Merry was wearing a velvet candy-striped waistcoat that the girls hadn't seen before. "We're in for a treat today!" he smiled. Then to Summer's astonishment, he danced a jig on the spot. She'd never seen him so excited! "Today is one of my favourite days of the whole year!" he continued. "And Candy Cove is one the most wonderful places in the whole kingdom."

Just then, a round and cheery-faced lady came bustling out of the Dandy Candies workshop. She was wearing a yellow dress and a large hat decorated with sweets. Under her arm she carried a pink candy cane that sparkled in the sunshine. "King Merry!" she cried in delight, hugging him. "Welcome to Candy Cove. Are you ready for the launch of The Sweet Princess?"

King Merry blushed beetroot red.
"I … um … er… Mrs Sherbet, it
is *always* a pleasure to
see you!"

"Girls, this is
Mrs Sherbet,"
said Trixi. "Mrs
Sherbet, I'd like
you to meet
Ellie, Summer
and Jasmine."

Mrs Sherbet
smiled at the
girls, her rosy cheeks
dimpling. "What an honour!" she cried.
"I've heard all about you."

She took a shiny pink boiled sweet from
her pocket and held it out on her hand.

Then she touched it with her candy cane. Sparkles danced around the sweet and suddenly three more appeared.

"Mrs Sherbet's candy cane is magical," Trixi explained. "It can create more of any of the sweet treats made in the magical Candy Cove workshops."

Mrs Sherbet handed the girls a sweet each. "This one is for you, King Merry," she said, handing him the fourth sweet.

The little king's eyes lit up. "Thank you, dear Mrs Sherbet." He unwrapped the sweet eagerly, but he wasn't looking at what he was doing and he popped the wrapper into his mouth and put the sweet in his pocket! "Oh dear," he said unhappily. "This isn't quite as nice as usual." He took the wrapper out of his mouth again and looked at it in surprise.

"The sweet is in your pocket," said Trixi, trying to cover up a giggle as she helped King Merry swap it.

"That's better," he said. "Delicious!"

"They taste like strawberries and lemonade!" Ellie said.

"Mmmmm! What happens at the launch ceremony, Mrs Sherbet?" Jasmine asked, her mouth full of the sweet.

"Well, King Merry and I will both say a magic spell, then he'll break a fizzy cola bottle against the side of the ship," replied Mrs Sherbet. "And then we'll be off, spreading happiness – and deliciousness! – throughout the Secret Kingdom." She glanced at her watch. "The launch will take place at noon when the Sweet Sea tide is at its highest. There's plenty of time before then for a tour of my very special ship. Would you like to look round?"

"Yes, please!" the girls chorused.

"I'll come and join you later, if you don't mind, Mrs Sherbet," King Merry said. "I've been worrying about the words

of the spell. So I'm going to stay here
and practise. Hmmmm, now how does it
go…" He unfolded the paper and began
to pace up and down, mumbling the
words in a low voice.

"I'll stay and help him," said Trixi,
winking at the girls. "Have a lovely time
on board The Sweet Princess."

"We will," the girls said. It was brilliant
being in the Secret Kingdom without
Queen Malice trying to ruin everything.
For once they could just have fun!

The girls followed Mrs Sherbet along
the narrow street to the harbour, where
candy-coloured boats bobbed gently on
the waves. In the midst of them all was
an old-fashioned sailing ship with a shiny
pink-and-green striped hull. Brightly
coloured sails flapped from masts made

from candy canes and upside-down ice cream cones, and the rigging was red liquorice. The whole ship was made out of sweets!

"It looks good enough to eat!" gasped Jasmine. She could hardly wait to go on board!

"It is," Mrs Sherbet replied proudly. "The ship is made from a humbug, and the sails are marzipan. Everything else…" She waved a hand towards the ship. "Well, you'll see when I show you round!"

"Have you seen the sea?" Jasmine asked her friends suddenly.

Ellie and Summer looked down at the water. "It's pink!" Ellie gasped.

As they hurried across the gangplank a big wave splashed up, showering them with pink seawater. Summer licked her lips and then laughed. "It tastes like cherryade," she said, astonished.

"Of course," Mrs Sherbet said, with a beaming smile. "Candy Cove is surrounded by the Sweet Sea. Everything is delicious here!"

Ship Surprises

Summer, Ellie and Jasmine gazed around the ship in amazement. The Sweet Princess's deck was piled high with delicious-looking treats in beautiful arrangements. Gnomes bustled about adding more sweets to the displays. Everywhere they looked they could see sparkling sweets and glittering goodies.

"Help yourself," said Mrs Sherbet. "My magic candy cane can replace anything you eat!"

"Don't we have to pay?" Summer asked, anxiously. "I mean, it is a shop."

"But it's a *magic* sweet shop!" Mrs Sherbet said with a grin. "You can take whatever you like, as long as you leave enough for everyone else to enjoy."

"Thank you," the girls chorused.

Excitedly, Summer reached for a purple sweet shaped like a dragon. As

she picked it up a little cloud of sherbet wafted out of its nose like a puff of smoke. Summer caught it on her tongue and laughed as it fizzed in her mouth.

Ellie chose a yummy-looking chocolate bar. "Mmmm! This tastes fantastic," she said, taking a huge bite that revealed layers of chewy nougat in every colour of the rainbow.

Jasmine helped herself to an iced biscuit shaped like a star. "Yummy!" she said, licking icing from the top. But no matter how much icing she licked off, more immediately appeared!

Summer sniffed deeply. "Mmmmm, I can smell marshmallows," she said.

"That's the marshmallow trampoline," beamed Mrs Sherbet, pointing to a giant pink cushion on the deck of the ship.

"Try it. It's wonderfully bouncy."

Jasmine kicked off her
shoes and leapt on
to it. She bounced
high into the
air, then turned
a somersault.
"Come and join
me!" she called
to Summer and
Ellie, but they'd
spotted a colourful
carousel filled with
lollipop animals and
were already running
towards it. Summer climbed
on to a red lollipop elephant and
Ellie sat behind her on a blue ostrich.

Jasmine ran over and climbed up onto

a green giraffe. The carousel began to turn and the lollipop animals moved smoothly up and down.

Over the carousel's jolly music,

Summer suddenly heard a giggle. "Did you hear that?" she asked, glancing at the others.

"What?" Jasmine said.

"I thought I heard someone laughing," said Summer. "It sounded as though it came from up in the sky."

They got off the carousel and looked around, but there was nothing to see except the tall masts, the furled sails and the bright blue sky.

Summer shrugged. "I can't see anyone. Maybe I imagined it."

Mrs Sherbet came over. "Would you like to see the rest of the ship? There's still half an hour before the launch."

"Yes, please," the girls replied eagerly.

Following Mrs Sherbet, they whizzed down a toffee slide to the lower deck.

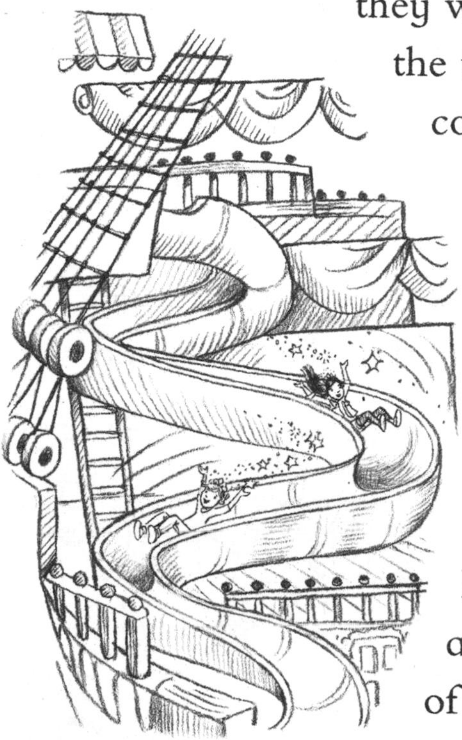

"Whee!" squealed Jasmine as
they whooshed down
the twisty, caramel-
coloured slide.

"Welcome
to the cake
cabin," said
Mrs Sherbet,
when they
got to the
bottom. She
led them under
a low arch made
of pretty fondant
fancies and into an
enormous room that stretched away in
every direction.

"The Sweet Princess seems really huge
now we're on board," said Jasmine.

"That's all part of the magic!" Mrs Sherbet replied with a smile. "We sail by magic, too. The Sweet Princess needs to get all around the kingdom in a week, or some people won't get any sweets or treats this year."

"Everything looks so delicious," said Ellie, looking around at the cakes and

licking her lips hungrily.

"Taste whatever you like!" Mrs Sherbet told her, gesturing with her candy cane. "I can always make more!"

The girls each took a cake and nibbled it as they followed Mrs Sherbet past columns made of macaroons and fondant statues of animals and birds. Twinkling rainbow hundreds and thousands covered the walls. The round

lollipop portholes let in dazzling sunshine
so the treats glowed and sparkled in all
different colours.

Mrs Sherbet led them into a room full
of pink candyfloss. "Yummy!" Jasmine
exclaimed. They eagerly pulled wisps
of candyfloss from the walls to taste it,
but when they tried to go on through
the room, they found their shoes were
stuck to the floor! Holding hands and
laughing, the girls pulled each other free
of the sticky candyfloss and followed Mrs
Sherbet into the next sweet-filled room.

Suddenly, Mrs Sherbet gasped. She
knelt down to examine a basket of
flying saucer sweets. Every single one
had a bite mark in it and the sherbet
was spilling out everywhere. "I can't
understand it," she said, shaking her head

in bewilderment. "The gnomes have gone ashore now so there's only the four of us on board. The Secret Kingdom Sweet Shop is for everyone to enjoy, but someone seems to have spoiled these sweets on purpose."

The girls exchanged worried glances – first a mysterious giggle and now someone was spoiling the sweets!

Mrs Sherbet touched the flying saucers with her candy cane and, with a sparkle, they grew whole again. "There. No harm done," she said. "But I think we should search the ship to make sure there's nobody hiding on board."

"Good idea," agreed Jasmine.

The girls followed Mrs Sherbet up some white-chocolate stairs and on to the deck. They looked all around but they didn't spot anyone.

"Let's head towards the front of the ship," suggested Ellie. They hurried past a bubbling hot-chocolate fountain, then skirted a huge swimming pool brimming with lemonade. Going up more steps, they found themselves on a small deck with a huge caramel steering wheel and an enormous butterscotch compass.

"There's nobody here," said Summer. She ran to the chocolate railing and looked across the whole ship. The deck below was completely deserted.

"Is this where you steer the ship, Mrs Sherbet?" asked Ellie.

"That's right," Mrs Sherbet replied. "If I want to head south, I choose S on the compass." She tapped it with her finger. Multi-coloured sparkles flew up into the air, forming glittery letters.

"Look, they're spelling out the names of places," Jasmine cried. "There's Lily Pad Lake and Wildflower Wood."

"And Fairytale Forest and Dolphin Bay," added Summer.

Just then, there was a clatter from up by the masts. The girls looked up and were horrified to see a huge crowd of Storm Sprites perched on the liquorice rigging. They gave high-pitched giggles as they flapped around the masts and sails. They *sounded* like Storm Sprites, but they *looked* different.

"What are they wearing?" Summer asked, squinting up at the sprites.

"They're dressed up in hats and funny clothes—" Ellie said.

"Like pirates!" Jasmine cried. "They're dressed like pirates!"

Pirate Sprites!

The Storm Sprites swooped down towards the girls, their bat–like wings flapping noisily. They were dressed up as pirates, with newspaper hats painted with lopsided Jolly Rogers. "We're the Candy Cove pirates," they crowed. "And this ship belongs to US!"

The naughty creatures dived down, waving cardboard swords. One flapped over Mrs Sherbet's head and grabbed her magic candy cane.

"Give that back!" Mrs Sherbet cried.

"Look at my special sparkly stick!" the

sprite cried proudly, meanly poking the other sprites with it.

"Mrs Sherbet's candy cane!" cried Jasmine. The sprites couldn't have stolen anything worse. "We have to get it back!" she whispered to the others.

Ellie and Summer nodded. As soon as the sprites realised that the cane had magical powers, they'd *never* give it back!

The girls dashed towards the sprite, but he flew up into the air. He settled on top of the highest mast and stuck his tongue out at them.

"Whatever can we do?" gasped Mrs Sherbet. "I can't launch the ship without my candy cane."

"I'll climb the rigging and get it back," Jasmine said bravely. But before she could start to climb, the sprite took off. "You can't catch me!" he jeered, flying high over the deck.

The girls jumped as high as they could, trying to grab the candy cane, but the sprite flapped back up onto the rigging with his friends. The other Storm Sprites laughed rudely and pulled silly faces. Then they began to sing:

"Yo ho ho and a bottle of pop.
You're too useless to make us stop.
Yo ho ho and a pirate's hat.
You're weedy girls and that is that!"

Then they snapped off the tops of the ice-cream-cone masts and started munching them greedily.

"What do you want?" Jasmine called up to the sprites. They had to persuade

the pirate sprites to give the cane back
or the ship couldn't be launched at
midday!

"We're here to have a feast!"
shouted a sprite who was
wearing a hat that was far
too big for him.

"Yeah!" sneered the
sprite with the candy
cane. "We're here to
eat everything up
and there's *nothing*

you can do about it!" He poked the candy cane at Jasmine. "And if you want this sparkly stick back, you'll have to come up here and get it!" he called. But as he twirled the cane around, it slipped out of his hands!

Jasmine ran forward, hoping to catch it, but it got caught on the liquorice rigging. As soon as the magic cane touched the liquorice, more red ropes appeared.

"Wow!" The Storm Sprites swarmed towards the cane, reaching for it eagerly. "Did you see that?" one of them cried. "It made *more* sweets." He grabbed the cane and tapped it on a sail. At once three new sails appeared. They flopped down on top of the sprites below, making them screech in alarm.

"Oh, no! Now we'll *never* get it back!"

groaned Mrs
Sherbet.

The sprite with
the candy cane
began to
fly around
the ship,
shrieking
gleefully
and tapping
everything he
could see. Sweets
multiplied so quickly that they spilt across
the deck. The lemonade pool overflowed,
and so many lollipop animals appeared
on the carousel that the base snapped
under their weight.

"They're ruining everything!" Summer
gasped, looking around in dismay.

Mrs Sherbet wrung her hands. "My poor ship," she groaned. "How will we ever launch it on time now?" Tears welled up in her eyes. "We have to leave at midday or we'll miss the tide and we'll never get right round the kingdom!"

Just then Trixi appeared, speeding between the greedy sprites on her leaf. The girls were so pleased to see their pixie friend! "What's happening?" she cried, her eyes wide with horror.

The girls quickly explained.

"Why have you come to Candy Cove?" Trixi shouted at the top of her voice. "You can visit the ship when it's travelling around the kingdom. Everyone is welcome!"

"Because we're *never* allowed to visit the Secret Kingdom Sweet Shop," one of them said grumpily.

"Queen Malice won't let us," added another sprite.

"So what are you doing here now?" asked Jasmine.

"We sneaked off when she was having a nap," the sprite said. His eyes lit up suddenly and he grinned round at his friends. "Come on, let's see what else we can eat below deck!"

"We've got to stop them," Summer gasped. They'd already wrecked the top deck. She couldn't bear to think of the rooms below deck being ruined, too!

"Can you use your magic to stop them, Trixi?" Ellie asked as the sprites flapped towards the toffee slide that led to the lower deck.

"I'll try," said Trixi. "But there are so

many of them, I'm not sure it will work."
She tapped her pixie ring and chanted:

"Pixie magic, stop these sprites
And make them leave without a fight."

Purple
sparkles came
whooshing
out of
her ring.
As they
surrounded
her, the
sparkles
changed her
clothes so Trixi was
wearing a tiny pirate
outfit! As they touched the pirate

sprites, their cardboard swords flew out of their hands. But most of the sprites dodged the sparkles.

"Ha ha," the sprites jeered through mouths crammed full of sweets. "We're the Candy Cove Pirates and you can't stop us!"

A Sticky Situation

"What are we going to do?" said Ellie in a worried voice. "It must be nearly time for the launch!"

The girls exchanged anxious looks. They had to find a way to get rid of the sprites, tidy up the ship *and* get Mrs Sherbet's candy cane back before midday so the ship could set sail.

"What about the candyfloss room?" Summer said suddenly. "We nearly got stuck there because the candyfloss is so sticky. If we can get the pirate sprites inside, perhaps they'll get stuck, too?"

"That's a great idea, Summer!" exclaimed Ellie. "But how can we do it? They won't listen to us."

"I know how!" Jasmine cried. "But we'll need disguises."

"I can help," said Trixi, zooming around the girls on her leaf.

"If Trixi disguises us as creatures who live in the Secret Kingdom, the pirate sprites won't be suspicious of us," Jasmine said. "We could look like..."

"Gnomes!" cried Ellie. "Candy Cove is full of them, so we won't look out of place. They'll never know it's us!"

"Brilliant!" Jasmine exclaimed.

"We could say we're going to take them around the ship and show them the tastiest treats?" Summer said. "We'll start with the candyfloss cabin and hope they get stuck in there!"

Mrs Sherbet looked more cheerful. "I think that might work," she said hopefully.

Trixi checked that none of the sprites were watching, then tapped her pixie ring and chanted a spell:

"Change the girls before my eyes
And give them each a gnome disguise."

Multi-coloured sparkles flew out of her ring and surrounded the girls. Summer, Ellie and Jasmine felt themselves shrinking, and their clothes began to change.

The sparkles faded and the girls grinned at each other. They looked exactly like gnomes, with long white beards and colourful suits and hats! Jasmine's hat was covered in swirls, Ellie's was stripy, and Summer's had a diamond

pattern. The girls looked at each other and laughed out loud.

"Everything looks bigger, even you, Trixi," Summer said. Her voice sounded much more squeaky than usual.

"We're about half our usual size," Jasmine pointed out. She scratched her chin. "I'm glad I don't always have a beard. It's itchy!"

"Let's go and speak to the Storm Sprites," said Summer. "Wish us luck!"

"Good luck," said Trixi and Mrs Sherbet together.

"We'll keep watch for any more pirate sprites," said Mrs Sherbet.

The girls hurried over to the lower deck, where the sprite were nibbling everything in sight.

"Roll up for the guided tour," called

Jasmine. "Only special guests are invited."

A few of the sprites turned to look at her. "What are you talking about?" one demanded rudely.

"It's an exclusive tour for very important guests," said Ellie. "So that they don't miss any of the delicious treats."

"I'm VERY important," said one of the sprites proudly.

"I'm more important than you," said another, barging the first one aside.

"There's room for all of you on our tour," Summer promised.

Soon all the pirate sprites were gathered excitedly around the girls.

The girls exchanged relieved glances. The first part of their plan seemed to be working.

"Follow me!" Jasmine said, rushing to the toffee slide and zooming down. She led the group down the passageway towards the candyfloss room. "There are fifty rooms on this deck." She had no idea if that was true, but she wanted to sound like a real tour guide.

Ellie joined in. "It takes ten minutes to walk from one end of the ship to the other," she told the Storm Sprites.

"And there are more than a thousand different types of sweets to be enjoyed," Summer added. She wanted to hurry the pirate sprites along, but every few steps they spotted a new treat, touched it with the candy cane to make loads more and then gobbled them all down.

At last they reached the door to the candyfloss room and Ellie threw it open. "Ta-da!" she cried. "The candyfloss room is the highlight of our tour."

The pirate sprites looked inside…but then they started to groan. "I've eaten too much," said one miserably.

"I feel sick," another complained.

"Me too," said a third, holding his tummy and moaning.

The girls looked at each other in horror. Suddenly, Summer had an idea.

"Fearless Pirate Ferdinand, the Terror of the High Seas, eats loads of candyfloss to make him brave," she said.

Jasmine winked at Summer. "So do Pegleg Percy and Hookhand Horace," she said, trying not to giggle.

The pirate sprites looked at each other in dismay, then a few took deep breaths and stepped into the room. "I'm the bravest pirate of all," said one. Reluctantly he pushed a wisp of candy floss into his mouth.

"No, I'm much braver than you," groaned another sprite, grabbing a sticky handful of candy floss.

One by one, the other pirate sprites stepped inside the sticky room.

"I'm the bravest pirate in the world," said another sprite, his cheeks bulging.

He tried to draw his sword to wave it at the other sprite, but found that his arm was stuck in the candyfloss. "Oh," he said weakly. "I can't move."

The other sprites tried to pull him free, but found that they were stuck, too.

"Oh no," wailed the sprite with the

candy cane. "We'll have to eat the candyfloss to get out." He took a bite, then groaned. "And I'm too full!" he wailed.

All over the room, the pirate sprites snuggled into the soft candyfloss, clutching their tummies.

Being careful not to touch any of the candyfloss, Ellie reached into the room and grabbed Mrs Sherbet's magical candy cane from the sprite. "I've got it!" she whooped. "Quick, let's get back on deck. There's not a moment to lose!"

Shipshape Again

Still disguised as gnomes, Jasmine,
Summer and Ellie sprinted back up onto
the main deck. Everything was such a
terrible mess!

"At least Mrs Sherbet can start putting
everything right now we've got her
candy cane," said Summer.

Ellie spotted Trixi and called out to her.

"You girls look so funny," the little pixie said, flying over on her leaf. "Did your plan to trap the sprites work?"

"Yes!" replied Jasmine, holding up the candy cane. "Now we just have to return the cane to Mrs Sherbet!"

"What are we going to do with the sprites?" asked Summer.

"I can help with that!" Trixi grinned. She tapped her pixie ring and chanted:

"These sprites can't fly,
their tums are sore.
Let stretchers bring them to the shore!"

Sparkles flew from the ring and swirled down to the lower deck. Moments later, glittering stretchers in all colours of the rainbow came whizzing out from the

lower deck, each carrying a pirate sprite.
They were still covered in sugary pink
wisps. Some of them were snoring loudly.

The stretchers sped away from the ship

and landed on the quay, where they
vanished, dumping the sprites on the
ground in a groaning heap. "I don't think
they'll be back," Trixi giggled.

She tapped her ring again and this time

sparkles whirled around the girls. "We're turning back to normal!" cried Summer.

In a twinkling they looked like themselves again. "That's better," said Jasmine. "That beard was really starting to tickle!"

"How long have we got before the launch, Trixi?" asked Ellie. There was so much to do to get the ship ready in time!

Trixi zoomed into the air on her leaf to check the time on the Candy Cove town hall clock. "Only five minutes," she said worriedly.

Mrs Sherbet was sadly sweeping half-eaten sweets over the side of the ship, but her eyes lit up when she spotted her candy cane.

"You've got it!" she called as she hurried towards them. "Thank you, girls.

I must get to work right away." She
hurried along the deck, touching her
candy cane to the broken sweets. Clouds
of pink sparkles whizzed out, magically
repairing the damage the pirate sprites
had caused. The girls ran along behind
her, arranging huge piles of sparkling

jelly tots, glistening gummy sweets and brightly wrapped toffees.

"Thank goodness Mrs Sherbet has her candy cane back!" said Summer. It looked as though the ship might be ready for the launch ceremony after all!

Trixi came zooming along, leaning forward on her leaf to make it fly fast. "It's nearly midday!" she cried. She sped away with the girls and Mrs Sherbet racing after her.

King Merry was waiting for them on the

quay, where a huge crowd of gnomes
and other magical creatures had gathered
to watch the launch. The little king was
hopping from foot to foot in excitement.
"Hurry!" he called when they appeared
on deck. "It's almost time!"

The girls ran across the gangplank and

on to the quay, with Trixi flying beside
them. "Can you remember the spell, Your
Majesty?" the royal pixie asked.

Before the king could reply, the clock
struck twelve. The girls watched Mrs
Sherbet take her place beside him.

"Doesn't the ship look brilliant?"
whispered Ellie. She could hardly believe
that it had been repaired so quickly.
Its pink-and-green stripes gleamed

brightly in the sunshine.

A trumpet sounded, then a group of gnomes in stripy sailor's shirts came skipping along the quay. They crossed the gangplank and took up positions on the deck of the ship.

King Merry and Mrs Sherbet joined
hands and began to chant the spell that
would send the Secret Kingdom Sweet
Shop around the kingdom:

"Set the sweetest tall ship sailing,
Let there be no storms or hailing,
Just a good breeze and lots of sun
As we bring joy to everyone!"

King Merry cleared his throat and
glanced nervously at Trixi, who gave him
an encouraging smile. "Friends," he said.
"We have come here today to launch
The Princess Sherbet."

"The Sweet Princess, Your Majesty,"
whispered Trixi.

"Yes, yes, of course." King Merry
blushed, then began again. "We have

come to launch The Sweet Princess and wish her well on her wonderful voyage."

Trixi handed him a fizzy cola bottle tied to a rope. He swung it at the ship and it smashed against the bow, sprinkling it with sugar sparkles. Then King Merry and Mrs Sherbet held hands and dashed across the gangplank. The girls and Trixi followed them back on to the ship.

"Hooray!" cheered the crowd. The trumpeter tooted as the ship drifted away from the quay. As Summer, Jasmine and Ellie waved to the crowd, the sails billowed and The Sweet Princess headed out to sea, bobbing gently over the waves. A school of flying fish appeared, their turquoise scales glinting in the

sunshine. They dived in and out of the water alongside the ship. Then the girls heard sweet music and spotted a mermaid harpist sitting on a rock near the harbour.

"What a brilliant send off!" Jasmine exclaimed.

"Thank goodness we got everything finished in time," said Summer.

"What will happen to the Storm Sprites?" asked Ellie. They were still lying in a groaning heap on the quay, clutching their tummies.

"They'll go back to Thunder Castle as soon as they feel well enough," Trixi said. "And you girls should probably go back home now too." Grinning, she added, "But would you like to come back tomorrow?"

"Yes please!" the girls chorused.

"I'll see you tomorrow at noon then," said Trixi.

The girls joined hands, ready for the spell that would carry them home. Trixi tapped her ring and chanted:

"Let magic sparkles fall like rain
And take our good friends home again."

Silver sparkles cascaded out of the ring. They fell all around the girls, just like silvery raindrops, then they began to spin and the girls felt themselves being lifted off their feet. "Bye, Trixi," they called. "See you tomorrow!"

A moment later they found themselves back in Summer's bedroom. "That was amazing!" exclaimed Ellie.

"Yes," agreed Jasmine. "It was brilliant!"

"I can't wait until tomorrow," Summer said. "I just know that sailing on The Sweet Princess is going to be a *delicious* adventure!"

Book
Two

Book
Two

Contents

Sailing the Sweet Sea

"Aha, me hearties!" cried Ellie. "Let's tickle all these pirates until they surrender!"

Ellie, Summer and Jasmine were at Summer's little brother's pirate birthday party, pretending to capture all his giggling friends.

The little boys squealed and ducked under the girls' outstretched arms.

"After them, shipmates!" Summer laughed, running after her youngest brother, Finn.

Her mum came over with a plate of food. "You make terrific pirates," she said.

The girls exchanged smiles. It was only

yesterday that they'd beaten some *real* pirates – the Candy Cove Pirates!

"Lunchtime, everyone," Summer's mum called out.

Jasmine glanced at the clock. "It's almost noon," she whispered excitedly. Yesterday the girls had had to deal with some very naughty Storm Sprites who had boarded the magical sweet ship, The Sweet Princess, and tried to eat all the delicious treats on board! The friends had worked with Trixi and Mrs Sherbet to trap the Storm Sprites in the candyfloss room so the ship could be launched on time for its one-week journey around the kingdom. Now, in just a few minutes, Trixi would magic them back to the Secret Kingdom so they could join in with the very special voyage!

"Do you mind if we go outside for a minute, Mum?" Summer asked. She knew time would stand still while they were in the Secret Kingdom, so they wouldn't miss even a second of Connor's birthday party, but they had to make sure that no one saw their pixie friend, Trixi, appear.

"Of course not," her mum replied.

Jasmine grabbed her backpack with the Magic Box inside it and the girls ran outside into the small garden next to the play centre. They darted behind a tree and Jasmine took out the Magic Box. As she set it on the grass, a riddle appeared in the mirror. Summer read it out eagerly:

"Our ship bobs on gentle waves
Where water's pink and clear.
Just say its name and you can come
And join our voyage here!"

The girls grinned at each other. "That's easy!" said Ellie.

"The Sweet Sea," they cried together.

Pink sparkles burst out of the box, then Trixi appeared, riding on her leaf. She was wearing the pirate outfit she'd magicked up yesterday.

"It's the perfect thing for a sea voyage!"
she laughed as they girls looked at her
costume. "We've already sailed down
the Jolly River to the Enchanted Palace,
where we dropped off lots of scrumptious
lemonade for King Merry's fountain and
lots of people came on board to try the
treats. Now we're back on the high seas."

The girls jumped up and held hands.
Trixi tapped her pixie ring and chanted:

"In the blink of an eye, or maybe less,
Take us to The Sweet Princess!"

A glittery, sweet-smelling cloud puffed
out of the ring, then twirled around the
girls, lifting them off their feet. "Here we
go!" gasped Summer.

A moment later the girls landed gently

on the deck of The Sweet Princess. "We're here!" Jasmine exclaimed excitedly. "And everything looks perfect!" The marshmallow trampoline and the lollipop carousel looked as good as new.

The lemonade pool sparkled in the sunshine, and above their heads the ship's marzipan sails flapped and billowed, sending The Sweet Princess skimming smoothly across the waves. All across the deck the gnome crew were working busily, hauling on red liquorice ropes to adjust the sails and turning the enormous caramel steering wheel.

"You'd never know the ship had been overrun with naughty pirate sprites yesterday," Ellie said happily.

"It's the perfect day for a seaside trip," smiled Jasmine.

Summer heard a splash and looked over the side of the ship into the pink water of the Sweet Sea. "Dolphins!" she cried.

The shimmering blue creatures were swimming alongside the ship, diving in and out of the water. "Oh, and look!" she gasped, pointing. Mermaids were swimming beside the dolphins. They waved and blew kisses to the girls, and the dolphins nodded their heads and clicked in greeting.

Mrs Sherbet came hurrying along the deck. She was wearing a pink-and-white striped dress with a wide skirt decorated with shiny sweet wrappers. "I thought I heard your voices," she cried happily.

 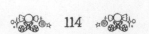

"Welcome!" called a voice and King Merry appeared on deck too. He was wearing a sailor's hat underneath his crown and holding a towering ice cream cone, with scoop after scoop of different flavours balanced on top of each other. It wobbled as King Merry raced along.

"Don't worry," Trixi whispered to the girls, "I've enchanted it so he can't drop it."

As King Merry reached them, Mrs Sherbet gently tapped his cone with her candy cane and three more enormous ice creams magically appeared in front of

Jasmine, Summer and Ellie.

"Thank you!" chorused the girls.

"Where is The Sweet Princess going next, Mrs Sherbet?" asked Ellie, taking a lick of her ice cream.

"Magic Mountain," the cheery lady replied. "The snow brownies need plenty of hot chocolate and marshmallows to enjoy as they play in the snow."

The girls exchanged excited looks. It had been ages since they'd seen their snow brownie friends!

"The imps from Cloud Island always come down when we stop at Magic Mountain," continued Mrs Sherbet. "They love my candyfloss."

"Thank goodness the pirate sprites haven't been back to scoff it all," said Jasmine, smiling with relief. Suddenly her smile faded as a black cloud covered the sun and an evil cackle filled the air.

"That's right!" cried a familiar mean voice. "*I'm* here instead."

The girls spun round in horror. "It's Queen Malice!" gasped Summer.

Admiral Malice

A chilly wind blew around The Sweet
Princess, making everyone shiver. Then
a spiky black ship appeared from behind
the curve of the island, its sails billowing
as it sped towards them.

"Thunder Yacht," whispered Ellie.

Queen Malice stood at the front of the
ship, holding her thunderbolt staff high.

Even from a distance the girls could see
she was wearing an enormous captain's
hat, pulled down low over her black
frizzy hair, and a black waistcoat over
her long dress. A pirate flag, showing
Queen Malice's face over
two huge crossed

thunderbolts, fluttered at the top of her ship's mast.

The gnomes came running over to stand with the girls and Mrs Sherbet. They huddled together fearfully as they watched Thunder Yacht approach.

King Merry's sailor's hat and crown wobbled dangerously as he shook his head. He waved his ice cream cone at Queen Malice. "It's no good you trying

anything, sister," he warned. "I won't allow any mean behaviour."

Queen Malice laughed nastily. "My silly sprites told me they'd sneaked off yesterday while I was involved in Very Important queenly business."

"The sprites said she was having a nap!" Ellie whispered indignantly. Summer and Jasmine stifled their laughter as the mean queen glared at them.

"I have made up my mind," the wicked queen continued, "that nobody should have sweet treats. They make people far too happy! So I am taking over this silly sweet ship!"

She pointed at The Sweet Princess and her Storm Sprites flew up into the air and hovered above Thunder Yacht. They were dressed in their pirate outfits again and

began pulling
rude faces and
sticking out
their tongues.
"We're taking
your ship!"
they jeered.
"And there's
nothing you can
do about it. The
Candy Cove Pirates are
back! Ha ha haaa!"

The girls stepped forward bravely.

"We won't let you!" Jasmine shouted.

"You can't have the ship," Trixi said to
Queen Malice fiercely. She turned to the
girls and lowered her voice. "And if it's
pirates she wants, we'll beat her at her
own game!" She tapped her ring and

whispered some magic words. A magical
whirlwind suddenly surrounded the girls.
As it spiralled away, the girls looked
down at themselves in amazement. They
were all dressed as pirates too! Summer
was wearing a white blouse with
billowing sleeves and a yellow skirt. Ellie

was dressed in striped shorts and leather boots, and Jasmine's outfit was a stripy tunic with a sparkly pink belt.

"Wow!" gasped Jasmine. She twirled round making her long black hair fly out. "Thanks, Trixi."

"Can the ship go any faster, Mrs Sherbet?" asked Summer. "Queen Malice won't be able to take over The Sweet Princess if she can't catch it!" Summer whispered to the others.

"I think so," replied Mrs Sherbet. She spoke quietly to two of the gnomes and they saluted smartly, then switched on the ship's cinnamon-powered propellers. Suddenly The Sweet Princess shot forward.

"Catch them!" roared Queen Malice. The Storm Sprites flew after the ship, their bat-like wings flapping furiously.

"Faster, you idiots!" Queen Malice screeched. "Don't let them get away!"

Looking back, the girls saw the pirate sprites speed up. More sprites were fluttering and scurrying around on the deck of Thunder Yacht. A moment later, Queen Malice's ship sped up, too.

"Oh no," groaned Ellie. She couldn't bear to think of the mean queen taking over Mrs Sherbet's ship. No one in the kingdom would have any sweets for a whole year! "We can't let Queen Malice catch us!" she cried.

The girls ran to help the gnomes let out the ship's marzipan sails. The Sweet Princess sailed even faster, cutting through

the water and leaving a choppy wake behind that made Queen Malice's yacht rock heavily from side to side.

Still Thunder Yacht came closer, but the sprites flying after them seemed to be getting tired. Ellie grinned at Jasmine and Summer. "I think we're going to get away."

"I hope you're right," said Summer nervously. She shivered as she remembered all the damage the sprites

had caused yesterday. If Queen Malice
managed to get aboard, things would be
much worse!

"It'll be OK," said Ellie, squeezing
Summer's hand. "Look, the sprites have
given up chasing us."

The sprites had settled back on the rigging of Queen Malice's ship.

"Thunder Yacht doesn't seem to be getting any closer, either," Jasmine said.

Suddenly they heard a bang and a strange whistling noise. "What's that?" asked Ellie, looking round anxiously.

Something round and black was whizzing through the air towards them. The girls stared, trying to see what it was. It hit one of the sails, tearing a hole in it, then dropped down on to the deck with a loud clang.

The girls gasped in horror. Thunder Yacht was firing at them!

Thunderballs

The ball hit the deck, flashing with blue light and crackling with electricity. "Look out, Your Majesty!" Jasmine shouted, as it rolled towards King Merry.

Too late. The ball hit his ankle. "Ouch!" he cried. Every hair on King Merry's head – even his beard – suddenly stood straight up on end!

"They're thunderballs!" the king gasped.

Jumping to avoid the crackling balls, the girls dashed over to help him as Mrs Sherbet hurried to repair the damaged sail with her candy cane.

More thunderballs came flying over, giving anyone they hit a nasty zap and leaving all the sails in tatters. No matter how fast she scurried around to repair them, Mrs Sherbet couldn't keep up with the damage. Without her sails, The Sweet Princess started to slow down.

"This is hopeless," said Jasmine. "Thunder Yacht is catching up!"

"We need to fight back," Summer cried.

"I've got an idea!" Ellie called. "Quick, follow me!"

She whizzed down the toffee slide to the lower deck with her friends and Trixi close behind her.

"Gather anything that will stop that ship!" Ellie called out.

"These will be good," said Jasmine, spotting some flying saucers. "Remember how the sizzling sherbet made King Merry sneeze?"

Trixi tapped her pixie ring and chanted:

"Flying saucers on the breeze,
Make the Storm Sprites cough and sneeze."

The flying saucers glittered brightly, then rose up and fell into a line behind the girls.

"Can you put a spell on these too, Trixi?" Summer asked, pointing to a basket of lemon drops. "So that when people eat them they stand still?"

"Lemon *stops*, coming right up!" Trixi nodded and performed another spell. The lemon drops flew up and joined the line.

"Let's get back on deck," cried Jasmine. They charged up the white-chocolate stairs with the sweets zooming after them.

Mrs Sherbet and the gnomes hurried over to them. Some of the gnomes had been hit by thunderballs and their beards crackled with static electricity.

"Quick! Grab as many sweets as you can!" Summer told them.

Everyone seized handfuls of flying saucers and lemon drops.

"Attack!" yelled Ellie.

They hurled flying saucers like frisbees at Thunder Yacht. The sweets split open in the air and a cloud of sherbet covered the pirates sprites, who began to cough and sneeze.

"Yay!" cheered the girls.

Next, they gathered up all the lemon drops into a net. They pulled it back, like a slingshot, and let it go. A volley of lemon drops flew at Thunder Yacht.

"Your silly sweets can't hurt us!" jeered the sprites, scooping up the lemon drops.

"Maybe the sprites won't eat them," Summer said nervously. "Because they were so greedy yesterday."

But soon yelps and cries of "help!" rang out from Thunder Yacht, as the pirate sprites gobbled the lemon drops and got stuck by Trixi's spell.

Their plan was working, but there was no time to celebrate. Thunder Yacht was still powering towards them. It was so close they could see Queen Malice on the deck. She was shouting orders and waving her staff around wildly so it fired off thunderbolts that zinged away in all directions.

"We need to stop them!" cried Ellie.

Jasmine spotted a display of flowers made from pink bubble gum. "Can we use this to trap the rest of the sprites?"

"Great idea," said Trixi. "Everyone, blow some bubbles!"

Breaking off chunks, everyone started

chewing and blowing huge pink bubbles.
Trixi tapped her pixie ring and sparkles
came out of it. The bubble-gum bubbles
rose into the air and started growing
bigger and bigger. They drifted into the
air towards Thunder Yacht and then—

POP!

The bubbles
exploded,
covering
Thunder
Yacht and
lots of the
sprites with
pink, sticky
goo.

"Hooray!"
everyone
cheered, as the

pirate sprites struggled to get unstuck.

But to the girls' horror, Queen Malice's ship kept advancing. Soon Thunder Yacht was right next to The Sweet Princess.

"Get that sweet ship!" yelled the bubble-gum covered sprites. They swung

across to The Sweet Princess on liquorice ropes, then jumped on to the deck.

"Go away, you horrid sprites!" yelled Jasmine bravely. "This is Mrs Sherbet's ship."

"Not any more!" the sprites giggled meanly. "Now there won't be sweets for anyone but US!"

Queen Malice cackled wickedly as she banged down her thunderbolt staff down on the deck of Thunder Yacht. A black gangplank appeared, making a walkway between the two ships.

"We've got to stop her," cried Ellie. The girls tried to push the gangplank into the water, but it was firmly stuck on with the horrid queen's magic.

Still laughing, Queen Malice began to slowly cross the gangplank. "Out of my

way!" she yelled. She pushed past the
horrified girls and stepped down on to

the deck of The Sweet Princess with a horrid cackle. "Ha ha ha!" she laughed. "This ship is mine!"

The Ruler of the Sea!

Ellie, Jasmine and Summer gasped as more and more pirate sprites stormed aboard the ship. The greedy sprites charged around the deck, knocking things over and taking huge bites out of everything they passed.

King Merry came puffing up to Queen Malice. "This is too much, sister," he said angrily. "You're stopping us from taking treats to our friends around the kingdom. You know how much everyone loves coming aboard and sharing in the fun."

"Fun?" sneered the wicked queen. "I'll tell you what's fun – being a pirate. You, brother, are no longer welcome on board *my* ship."

"*Your* ship?" King Merry gasped.

Queen Malice beckoned to her sprites and they flapped over, waving cardboard swords at poor King Merry. The queen's dark eyes glinted wickedly as she looked round at them. "Prepare the plank!" she commanded.

Hooting with laughter, the pirate sprites tore up a plank of chocolate caramel from the ship's deck. They set it with one end jutting out over the sea, and stuck the other end to the ship with icing.

The girls stared at each other in horror. "She's going to make him walk the plank!" Summer realised.

"We won't let you do that," Jasmine said, stepping in front of King Merry. Summer and Ellie stepped forward too, protecting the little king.

"Just you try and stop me," cackled Queen Malice. She thumped her thunderbolt staff on the deck and suddenly a black liquorice rope whizzed through the air like a lasso. Spinning round and round, it tied Summer, Jasmine and Ellie tightly to the ship's main mast. The girls struggled against the liquorice lashings, but they couldn't escape.

"Dearie me, help them!" King Merry cried in alarm.

But with another thump of her staff, a huge bubble-gum bubble surrounded the gnome crew and another tiny bubble trapped Trixi. "See how *you* like being stuck," Queen Malice cackled nastily.

Snatching a cardboard sword from one

of the pirates, Queen Malice prodded the little king and forced him to step on to the plank.

"Don't worry," King Merry said bravely. "The friendly sea creatures will rescue me. Look!" he pointed to where a group of dolphins and mermaids were staring up at the boat anxiously.

"Is that so?" With a horrible cackle, the queen raised her staff and brought it crashing down on the ship's deck. A thunderbolt flew out and as it touched the sea, the dolphins and mermaids vanished. In their place, glittering triangular fins appeared. They circled round beneath the end of the plank.

"Sharks!" gasped Ellie. "Trixi, you have to help him!"

"But there aren't any sharks in the

seas around the Secret Kingdom!" the pixie cried, desperately trying to pop the bubble-gum bubble around her.

"There are *now*," Queen Malice said

coldly, "because I rule the sea!" She poked King Merry with the sword again and he took a shaky step forward on the plank, his feet sinking a little way into the gooey caramel. "That's right," she said. "Keep going. Only two more steps and you'll be swimming with the sharks!" She threw back her head and cackled loudly, setting her hat wobbling.

"Can you get rid of the sharks, Trixi?" whispered Summer. She could hardly bear to watch as King Merry shuffled nearer and nearer to the end of the plank.

The little pixie shook her head sadly. "Queen Malice's magic is much stronger than mine so I can't undo her spell. But…" Her face lit up. "Wait, there is something I can do!"

"Quick!" Jasmine cried. "King Merry's nearly at the end of the plank."

There was a *pop!* as Trixi finally managed to burst the bubble that she was trapped inside.

The king was standing with his toes jutting out over the sea. He stared down at the sharks anxiously. "One more step," cackled Queen Malice, prodding the king again.

"Quick, Trixi!" Jasmine shouted.

But it was too late. The girls watched

in horror as King Merry toppled off the
plank and went tumbling down towards
the hungry sharks.

A Lucky Escape

Summer, Ellie and Jasmine cried out as King Merry fell. But just in time Trixi tapped her pixie ring and chanted:

"Stop the king from getting wet
And catch him in a safety net."

Turquoise sparkles fizzed out of her ring and a net appeared just below the plank. To the girls' relief, King Merry landed safely in it.

The sharks leapt out of the sea, biting furiously, but King Merry was just out of reach. The disappointed sharks dove back into the sea with a huge splash.

"Well done, Trixi," sighed Summer.

But the little pixie looked very worried. "My magic won't last long," she said. "We've got to come up with a plan for getting rid of Queen Malice and her pirate sprites, fast!"

Luckily, Queen Malice was too busy bossing people around to notice that Trixi had escaped and saved King Merry.

"You!" Queen Malice said, jabbing her staff towards Mrs Sherbet. "Get busy repairing this ship! I want it looking as good as new!"

Mrs Sherbet reluctantly started repairing the damage that Thunder Yacht had caused, while Queen Malice stomped downstairs to inspect The Sweet Princess's lower decks.

"Can you cast a spell and set us free,

Trixi?" Ellie whispered.

Trixi shook her head. "Queen Malice's magic is too strong," she sighed. The girls struggled against the liquorice rope binding them to the mast. But it wouldn't budge.

Summer sighed. "I don't really like liquorice, but I can only think of one way to escape…"

"We have to eat our way free!" Ellie said with a giggle.

The girls bent their heads and started nibbling through their bindings.

A few pirate sprites noticed what they were doing.

Summer winked at Jasmine and Ellie. "Yummy!" she said through a chewy mouthful of liquorice. "This is sooo tasty! I'm glad we have it all to ourselves."

"No you don't!" said one sprite greedily. "It's our ship now, so we can eat whatever we want!" He came over and started to chomp at the liquorice.

In no time at all, the sprites had gobbled through the ropes. Summer, Jasmine and Ellie were free!

Ellie suddenly had another idea. "Does Mrs Sherbet's candy cane make copies of *any* sweets, Trixi?" she asked.

"Yes. Why?" replied the little pixie.

"Have you got a plan?" Summer asked hopefully. She and Jasmine leant in close to Ellie so they wouldn't be overheard.

"The Sweet Princess is made from one huge, hollowed out peppermint," said Ellie in a low voice. "So if Mrs Sherbet tapped it with her candy cane, she could make more ships."

"How will that help?" asked Jasmine, sounding puzzled.

"With more ships, we should be able to fight Thunder Yacht!" Ellie explained excitedly.

"That's a brilliant idea!" exclaimed Jasmine. Trixi flew on her leaf to Mrs Sherbet and whispered in her ear. The kind lady nodded and went across to speak to her gnome helpers. Looking like she was concentrating hard, she pointed her candy cane first at the bow and then at the stern of the ship. She tapped each of the ship's sides and suddenly zillions of sea-green sparkles appeared. They swirled around The Sweet Princess, making the air shimmer, then there was a brilliant flash of light. The girls blinked, then stared in delight. Three exact copies

of the Sweet Princess bobbed on the sea
next to them!

"What was that?" demanded Queen
Malice, coming back on deck. She
whirled round and her mouth fell open
in shock. "How did you get free?" she
screeched. "And where did those ships
come from?"

Trixi quickly tapped her pixie ring, and liquorice ropes unfurled from the rigging. "You three girls need to take command," she told them. "There's one ship for each of you."

Jasmine grabbed a rope. "Quick, get aboard the other ships!" she called.

"Let's surround Thunder Yacht," said Summer. "Then Queen Malice will have no choice but to surrender and leave us alone!"

"Captain Summer, Captain Ellie and Captain Jasmine to the rescue!" Ellie said with a grin.

Three Captains!

"Stop them!" Queen Malice screeched as she and her sprites raced towards the girls.

Jasmine grabbed a rope and swung through the air to the furthest ship. "Whee!" she yelled happily.

"Don't be scared, Ellie," said Summer reassuringly. "You can do it."

Ellie looked down at the sea below
with a gulp. She hated heights! As Queen
Malice ran closer, Ellie nodded bravely,
then clung to the rope and swung over
to the second ship with her eyes shut.

Finally, Summer swung across, landing on the bridge of her own ship. The gnomes followed them.

"Please turn us round so we're facing The Sweet Princess," called Jasmine to her gnome crew.

"Aye, aye, Captain," they said, heaving on ropes to change the angle of the sails.

"Sail round to the other side of The Sweet Princess," Summer commanded the gnomes on her ship.

The gnomes saluted, then spun the steering wheel. The ship began to edge round behind the original sweet ship.

"Steer towards Thunder Yacht," Ellie ordered. The gnomes turned her ship round, then sailed towards Thunder Yacht.

In hardly any time at all, the three new ships had moved into position and the original Sweet Princess was surrounded.

"Give up, Queen Malice," Jasmine
called out loudly.

"Never!" cackled the queen. "You
girls are no match for the Candy Cove
Pirates. Storm Sprites – get them!"

But Mrs Sherbet pointed her candy cane at Queen Malice. "You've been on my ship for quite long enough!" she shouted fiercely.

She strode towards Queen Malice so forcefully that the horrid queen backed away, stepping down the deck towards where the hot-chocolate fountain was.

"How dare you speak to me like that?" Queen Malice shrieked. She raised her thunderbolt staff menacingly.

But Mrs Sherbet was quicker. She took another step towards Queen Malice and plunged her candy cane into the hot-chocolate fountain. The chocolate bubbled and frothed as the candy cane magically made more of it. Then a huge wave of chocolate whooshed out of the

fountain – and over Queen Malice!
"Aargh!" spluttered Queen Malice.
"I HATE chocolate!"
The Storm Sprites
stared at the queen,
trying not to laugh.
Jasmine glared at
them sternly from
her ship. "You're
next, sprites," she
yelled. "Ready the
torpedoes!"
"Grab all
the gumballs!"
Summer shouted.
"Collect the
popping candy!" Ellie
called. "Get ready to fire!"
The sprites looked at the three ships

and the fierce girls and threw down their
pirate hats, waistcoats, and cardboard
swords. "Let's get out of here," they
squawked.

"I'm fed up with getting covered in
sticky stuff anyway," said one.

"And tired of feeling sick,"
added another.

They flapped
weakly back
towards
Thunder
Yacht.

"Come
back!" Queen
Malice ordered,
wiping chocolate from her face. She
stomped across the deck after them, but
her foot skidded. With a shriek she slipped

over, falling to the deck and knocking
over a barrel full of rainbow sprinkles.

When she scrambled back to her feet,

the mean queen was covered in chocolate and sprinkles from head to toe.

Jasmine, Ellie and Summer couldn't help bursting into laughter.

"I'll be back," Queen Malice yelled.

"Just you wait and see!" She put her soggy hat on her head, then she hurried over the gangplank, back to Thunder Yacht.

The girls jumped up and down with excitement. "We did it!" cheered Jasmine. "We defeated the Candy Cove pirates!"

The Luckiest Girls
in the World

Finally, the three captains gave the orders
to turn their ships around and soon they
reached the original Sweet Princess. The
girls and the gnomes swung back across
to Mrs Sherbet's ship.

"Oh no," gasped Summer as they looked around the deck in dismay. Queen Malice's attack had left the sails in tatters, the chocolate railings snapped and the lollipop portholes smashed. The sweet ship was in ruins again.

Suddenly, they heard a voice muttering, "Dearie, dearie me!"

"King Merry!" cried Summer. She felt awful – she'd forgotten all about him!

The girls ran to the side of the ship. Now Queen Malice had gone, her sharks had too, but the net was still hanging under the plank. They hurriedly hauled it up on deck and untangled the little king.

"Thank you," he said as they helped him to his feet and straightened his sailor hat and crown. "If it hadn't been for you, Malice would have stopped Mrs Sherbet

from sailing around the kingdom."
He shook his head sadly. "I *do* wish my
sister wasn't such a bother."

Mrs Sherbet came over, beaming.
"Thank you so much, girls. Now that
Queen Malice has gone, we can repair
the ship again."

As Mrs Sherbet hurried around,
touching damaged parts of the ship with
her magic candy cane, the girls and the
gnomes tidied the decks and arranged
piles of sweets into pretty displays. Soon
the ship was looking as good as new.

"Now we can continue our voyage,"
Mrs Sherbet said. "I'm sure everyone is
wondering what's happened to us."

"What about the other ships?" Ellie
asked, pointing to the three copies of
The Sweet Princess.

"We'll use them too!" Mrs Sherbet said with a grin. "The gnomes can sail them in different directions. That way we'll still be able to deliver sweets to every part of the Secret Kingdom this week."

Once the gnomes had boarded the new ships, Mrs Sherbet signalled to them to loosen The Sweet Princess's sails, setting the ship skimming swiftly along.

"I can see Magic Mountain," Jasmine said after a few minutes, pointing to its pink snow cap. Snow brownies were streaming down the mountain and waving excitedly as the ship drew close to the shore.

Some were already on the beach and as soon as the gnomes pushed out the gangplank they came aboard.

"Welcome!" Mrs Sherbet cried. She

began handing out mugs of steaming hot
chocolate from the fountain, topped with
wonderfully fluffy marshmallows and

swirls of sparkling cream.

Next, baskets heaped high with marshmallows and drums of chocolate powder came floating up the stairs to the deck. "That smells heavenly," said Summer, sniffing deeply.

The girls heard voices above their heads. Looking up they saw excited cloud imps bouncing down from the clouds and on to The Sweet Princess. "Hello, girls!" they cried, hugging Jasmine, Summer and Ellie tightly, then they jumped on to the lollipop roundabout and whooped happily as it whizzed round and round.

"I'll send messages to let everyone know we've arrived," said Trixi. She tapped her ring and called out:

"Send word to our friends, far and near,
To tell them Mrs Sherbet's here!"

Red sparkles came whooshing out of the ring, then shot away from the ship.

Suddenly, the girls heard splashing in the water nearby. Mermaids were swimming towards them. Their long hair floated around them and their colourful tails twinkled brightly in the sun. Behind them swam the ice mermaids and lots of glittery blue dolphins.

"Hello, everyone," the girls called, waving furiously.

More and more magical creatures streamed on to the ship. Pixies flew aboard on their leaves, and elves, dressed in their finest clothes, came skipping

across the gangplank. Everyone chatted excitedly as they explored the wonders of The Sweet Princess and sampled the amazing sweets.

"I suppose it's time for us to go," Jasmine said sadly.

"We've got another party waiting for us back home," Summer said. "Connor's

pirate birthday party!"

"I'm glad there won't be any *real* pirates there," giggled Ellie.

"We'll be on our way soon, too," said Mrs Sherbet. "We're sailing to Dolphin Bay next."

As the girls stood up, King Merry hurried over to hug them goodbye. There were cookie crumbs in his beard and a smudge of chocolate on his nose. "How can I ever thank you girls enough for saving The Sweet Princess?"

he said with a smile.

"I think we've had our reward," Jasmine said, patting her tummy contentedly. "And it was delicious!"

Trixi flew over and the girls joined hands, ready for their journey home. "There might be one more sweet surprise for you when you get back," the little pixie said mysteriously.

"What is it?" asked Jasmine.

Trixi giggled. "That would be telling." She gave them all a hug, then tapped her pixie ring and chanted:

"It's time to say a fond goodbye
To our dear friends. Now let them fly!"

Multi-coloured sparkles poured out of the ring and spun around the girls.

"Goodbye," they called, squeezing each other's hands tightly.

A moment later they found themselves

in the play centre's garden. "What a brilliant adventure!" exclaimed Jasmine. She put the Magic Box back into her backpack.

"I wonder what Trixi's sweet surprise is," Summer said as they went inside. Then she stopped and stared. Her mum was carrying Connor's birthday cake over to the lunch table. Summer had helped her make it and it was shaped like a pirate ship sailing on a sea of blue icing. But something was different – tiny figurines had appeared on the ship! "Look at those figures," Summer whispered. "They weren't there before."

"That's Mrs Sherbet with her candy cane," said Ellie, spotting a lady in a striped dress standing on the top deck.

"And there are gnomes too," Jasmine

cried. "And mermaids and dolphins swimming in the water."

The girls exchanged a secret smile. "Trixi must have added them,"

exclaimed Summer happily.

"With so many Secret Kingdom friends, we really are the luckiest girls in the world!" Ellie said with a smile.

Can Ellie, Summer and Jasmine
stop Queen Malice in their
next adventure

Sparkle Statue

Read on for a sneak peek...

A Magic Message

Ellie Macdonald concentrated hard as
she made the final touches to the pixie
she was painting. She added a shimmer
of glitter paint to the green ring on the
pixie's finger and sat back. "Finished!" she
said happily.

Summer Hammond and Jasmine Smith,
her two best friends, looked up. They
were all painting pictures for a display at

Honeyvale Library. Summer was drawing a unicorn and Jasmine had almost finished a mermaid.

"Oh, wow, Ellie! That's brilliant," said Summer. "It looks just like Trixi."

Ellie grinned. "It's much easier to paint a pixie when you're friends with one!"

The three girls giggled. They shared an amazing secret — they actually knew real pixies, unicorns and mermaids! They looked after the Magic Box, which could take them to an amazing place called the Secret Kingdom, where all kinds of magical creatures lived. Their best friends there were King Merry, the land's kind ruler, and Trixibelle, his royal pixie.

Summer sighed. "I might have seen lots of unicorns, but my picture still looks more like a camel!"

"And my mermaid is nowhere near as beautiful as a real mermaid," Jasmine said, showing her picture to Ellie. "What should I do?"

"Her face is really pretty," Ellie said. "But her purple tail doesn't look quite right…" She studied the painting. "I know! Why don't you add some different colours to the scales on her tail to make them shimmer?"

"Good idea," said Jasmine. "I'll try that."

"What about my unicorn, Ellie?" Summer asked eagerly.

Ellie pointed at the unicorn's back with her paintbrush. "Try picturing a unicorn in your head. Their backs curve down, not up." As she traced a curve in the air above Summer's picture, a blob of glitter paint fell off her brush and landed on the unicorn's tummy. "I'm so sorry!" she gasped.

"Don't worry," said Summer. "I can start again."

"No, don't do that," Ellie said quickly. "You can use the glitter to make your unicorn glow. Like this——" She blended the glitter into the unicorn's pale pink tummy and added some to its mane and legs. Then she handed the brush to Summer. "Here, you try."

"My mermaid looks better already," said Jasmine, smiling at her picture. "You're so good at art, Ellie."

"We're all good at different things. You're amazing at singing and dancing," Ellie replied.

Jasmine grinned. "And Summer's

brilliant with all kinds of animals – even magical ones!"

"Oh, I miss the Secret Kingdom," Ellie said longingly. "It's been ages since we had an adventure there. Should we check the Magic Box? There might be a message from Trixi and King Merry. Did you bring it, Summer?"

"Of course!" Summer picked up her bag from the floor and handed it to Ellie.

Ellie was just about to open the drawstring top when her little sister, Molly, came running into the kitchen. Ellie hastily covered the bag with her arms.

"Look at my painting!" Molly cried. She held up a drawing of a lopsided stick figure, covered in glitter.

"It's really good, Molly," Summer said

encouragingly. "What is it?"

"It's a fairy, silly!" said Molly, as if Summer should have known. She waved it around so that the glitter caught the rays of sun streaming in through the kitchen window. "Look at it sparkle!"

As Ellie leaned down over the backpack, her eyes were caught by another sparkle – coming from inside Summer's bag! She caught her breath and opened the drawstring top just a little way. The wooden box inside was glowing – there must be a message for them! She hastily shut the bag. The Secret Kingdom had to be kept a secret, so they couldn't look in front of Molly.

"You know what, Mol?" she said. "I think you should paint a big, glittery yellow sun on your picture and maybe add some really sparkly birds in the sky."

"More glitter?" Molly asked eagerly.

"Yes, lots more," said Ellie, nodding hard. "I have some special glitter gel pens in my bedroom you can borrow." She saw Summer and Jasmine looking at her as if she'd gone mad. Ellie knew her little sister would make a mess, but it was worth it if it meant she and her friends could go on an adventure in the Secret Kingdom! "Make your picture really *glow*," she said, winking at her friends and nodding her head down towards Summer's bag.

Instantly their faces lit up and she knew they'd understood.

"Yes, add loads more glitter!" Jasmine said happily.

Molly skipped off to Ellie's room.

As soon as the kitchen door shut behind her, Summer and Jasmine jumped to their feet. "Is there a message for us?" Jasmine asked breathlessly.

"Yes!" Ellie pulled open the bag, revealing the box glowing inside. Golden light shone out into the kitchen as words swirled across the mirrored lid.

They knelt down on the floor and Summer took out the Magic Box.

Jasmine read out the message.

"To my friends, I send a magic invite
To celebrate art that sparkles so bright.
Find statues and paintings and all kinds of fun,
In a place full of beauty for everyone!"

As Jasmine finished speaking, the box

opened and a map floated out.

But Ellie wasn't looking at the map. Something else had caught her eye. "Look at these!" she exclaimed in delight, peering into the open Magic Box.

Summer and Jasmine looked over her shoulder. Inside the Magic Box there were four friendship bracelets. One was purple, one was hot pink, one was yellow and one – a very tiny one – was green. They each had a pretty silver charm attached to them.

"Friendship bracelets!" said Jasmine in surprise.

Summer carefully lifted the friendship bracelets out of the Magic Box. "Do you think they're for us?"

"Well, they're in our favourite colours. Oh and look!" Ellie held up the tiny bracelet. "This little one would be just right for Trixi," said Ellie.

Summer examined the silver charms. The charm on the pink bracelet was a musical note, the charm on the purple bracelet was a paintbrush, the yellow bracelet had a pawprint charm and the tiny green one had a leaf charm. "They must be for us!" she said.

Read

Sparkle Statue

to find out what
happens next!

Secret Kingdom

Look out for the next sparkling series!

Sparkle Statue

ROSIE BANKS

Melody Medal

ROSIE BANKS

Pet Show Prize

ROSIE BANKS

Twinkle Trophy

ROSIE BANKS

Queen Malice has stolen Jasmine, Ellie, Summer and Trixi's special talents! Can the girls give the four talent awards and get them back before Talent Week is over?

Pirate Puzzle!

The Storm Sprites are attacking The Sweet Princess! How many iced biscuits can you find in the picture below?

Secret Kingdom

Competition!

Would you like to win a Secret Kingdom goody bag?

All you have to do is decorate a dazzling pirate hat! You can use sweet wrappers, coloured paper or sparkles — anything to make it fit for a Candy Cove Pirate!

How to enter:

✶ Visit www.secretkingdombooks.com
✶ Click on the competition page at the top
✶ Print out the pirate hat activity sheet, and decorate it!
✶ Take a picture of yourself in your hat and follow the instructions to upload it, getting a parent or guardian to help you.

Three lucky winners will receive a special Secret Kingdom goody bag full of sweet treats and activities.

Alternatively, send postal entries to:
Secret Kingdom Candy Cove Pirates Competition
Orchard Books, 338 Euston Road, London, NW1 3BH

Don't forget to add your name and address.

Good luck!

Closing date: 30th September 2015

Secret Kingdom

Keep all your dreams and wishes safe in this gorgeous Secret Kingdom Notebook!

Includes a party planner, diary, dream journal and lots more!

Out now!